First published 1985 by
Deans International Publishing
Copyright © 1985 Victoria House Publishing Ltd.
This edition published 1989 by
Colour Library Books Ltd,
Godalming, Surrey, England.
ISBN 0 86283 662 X
All rights reserved

Printed in the German Democratic Republic

LITTLE OWL'S
BEDTIME
STORIES

Written by Lis Taylor
Illustrated by Colin Petty

Colour Library Books

Contents

Little Owl's Birthday Surprise

Little Owl yawned and stretched his wings. He tried to remember why today was special. Of course! It was his birthday.

He leapt out of bed, dressed as fast as he could and raced down to the kitchen. But no one was there, and there was no breakfast either. Well, how rotten of them! Fancy leaving him all alone on his birthday! He went to visit the Squirrels.

"Yoo hoo! Mrs Squirrel!" he called but no one was there either. "What a miserable birthday!" thought Little Owl. "I know, I'll go to my favourite place, the old oak tree."

As he flew towards it he noticed something big and square and brown resting on the lower branches.

"Why, it's a tree house!" he cried. "Who's built a house in *my* tree? I'll certainly find out!"

He landed and poked his head angrily round the door. There they all were—Mr and Mrs Owl, his sister Tootie and the Squirrel family.

"Surprise, surprise!" they called. "Happy birthday, Little Owl!"

"But whose house is this?" asked Little Owl, very puzzled.

"It's yours," said Mr Owl. "Your very own tree house!"

"Yippee!" shouted Little Owl. "I'm not having such a bad birthday after all!"

The Painting Competition

There was a big crowd round the oak tree in the school playground. Everybody was talking excitedly about the notice that Mr Mole had pinned to the tree:

PAINTING COMPETITION
FIRST PRIZE—A BIG JIGSAW PUZZLE

"I'm going in for it!" said Little Owl to his sister. "Are you, Tootie?"

"I'd really love to win a jigsaw," said Tootie sadly, "but I'm hopeless at painting."

"Have a go," said Little Squirrel kindly. "You might surprise yourself."

So Tootie went home and got out her paints and a big piece of paper. She laid them out at the foot of their tree and looked at all the lovely bright colours in their pots.

She dipped her brush in the blue paint and—whoops!—the pot tipped over. There was paint all over her paper!

"Oh no!" wailed Tootie. "It's spoiled!"

Just then a big gust of wind took hold of the paper and blew it away. It landed on a pile of sycamore leaves. Tootie ran to fetch it, but the wind caught it up again and dropped it on to Mr Squirrel's heap of chestnuts in their prickly green shells.

Before she could grab it, the wind whisked it away once more and this time it stuck to the bark of the Owls' tree. Tootie peeled it off and was surprised to see the beautiful pattern made by the leaves, the prickles and the bark.

Mrs Owl had popped down to see how she was getting on.

"What a clever idea!" she said.

Tootie didn't tell her how it had happened. She just took her painting to school and pinned it up with the others.

Mr Mole judged the paintings at lunchtime. Everyone hurried back early to see who had won. Tootie couldn't believe her eyes when she saw a red rosette beside her painting.

"First prize to Tootie," said Mr Mole, handing her the jigsaw. "A very good idea!"

Tootie just smiled.

Locked Out

It was baking day at Mrs Bunny's house. She had made four loaves of bread, a walnut cake, a carrot and banana pie, and a big batch of seed buns.

"Phew!" said Mrs Bunny, as she put the last of the seed buns in the oven. "It is hot in this kitchen. I'll just go out into the garden for a breath of fresh air while these are cooking."

She was chatting to her neighbour Mrs Hoppit when there was a sudden gust of wind and bang! Mrs Bunny's front door blew shut.

"Oh no!" she cried. "I'm locked out and my seed buns are cooking. They'll be burnt if I don't get back in quickly!"

There was a little window open, but Mrs Bunny was too big to climb through. Mrs Hoppit tried, but she was too big as well.

"What are you doing?" called Mrs Mouse. When they explained she said she would try to climb through the window, but she couldn't squeeze through either.

"You'll have to call out the fire brigade," she said. "I was going that way so I'll pop in and tell them."

"Thank you," said Mrs Bunny. "Oh my buns! They *must* be burnt by now!"

"What's the matter, Mrs Bunny?" called Percy Woodpecker, who was on his way home from school.

Percy tried the window, but he wasn't a good shape for it, really. Little Squirrel was passing so she tried, then Little Bunny arrived and Tootie Owl had a go too. No one could get through.

Just then Little Mouse came by.

"If anyone can get through, Little Mouse can," said Percy.

But even Little Mouse was too big. Mrs Bunny started to cry.

"My poor buns will be burnt to cinders. And if the fire brigade doesn't get here soon I should think the oven will catch fire too. Then my nice little house will burn down."

Poor Mrs Bunny sobbed so much that she hardly noticed the ting-a-ling of the firemen's bell as the fire engine raced to the gate.

"Don't you worry, Mrs Bunny," said the chief fireman, kindly. "We'll soon have this sorted out. You just dry your eyes and then we'll see what we can do."

Mrs Bunny reached into her apron pocket and pulled out her handkerchief. As she did, something fell to the ground with a tinkle.

"Look!" cried Little Bunny. "It's the front-door key! It was in your pocket all the time!"

Everyone burst into laughter and Mrs Bunny went very red. But she soon cheered up when she got inside. The seed buns weren't burnt—they were just ready to eat, nice and hot from the oven. So they all enjoyed them with a good cup of tea.

The Easter Egg Hunt

"Let's have an Easter egg hunt this year," suggested Little Owl at school one day. "We'll hide eggs all over the wood and then we'll look for them."

"Good idea," said Little Squirrel. "You can be in charge, Little Owl."

Little Owl was quite pleased at being in charge. He collected money from everyone to pay for the eggs and a few days before the hunt he went to Hollyholt Stores.

"Have you any eggs that we can use for our hunt?" asked Little Owl.

Mrs Badger lifted down several jars that held tiny Easter eggs, some coated in sugar and some made of jelly. Little Owl chose chocolate eggs, and Mrs Badger wrapped them up.

"I must put them in a safe place," he thought on the way home. "Somewhere where I won't be tempted to eat them."

On the morning of the hunt Little Owl finished his breakfast as quickly as he could.

"Before you start hiding your eggs, please will you wind the clock for me?" asked Mrs Owl, as Little Owl got up from the table. "It will stop altogether if it isn't wound soon."

But Little Owl wasn't really listening. He was trying to remember where he had put the eggs. He opened a cupboard in the kitchen, but they weren't there. "Maybe I put them in the wardrobe," he thought, but they weren't there either.

He was still looking when his friends arrived. Poor Little Owl, he daren't tell them he'd lost the eggs. They were sure to think that he had eaten them!

"Can we start hunting yet?" asked Little Mouse, excitedly.

"Um. Er, yes I suppose so," said Little Owl, who couldn't think what to do.

He sat on the doorstep watching them all rushing around searching for the eggs.

"Oh dear," he thought miserably. "They're bound to find out soon and then whatever will I say?"

He thought about tiptoeing away and hiding somewhere until they stopped being cross with him, but as he was about to do so Little Bunny ran up.

"Where are all these eggs?" he asked. "I haven't found a single one—and nor has anyone else. I think it's a trick!"

By now there was quite a crowd around Little Owl and they were all shouting, "Where are the eggs?" and, "It's not fair". Little Owl was just wishing he knew how to make himself invisible when a voice called out to him. It was Mrs Owl, and she sounded cross.

"I asked you to wind the clock this morning, but you forgot and now it's stopped. You'd better set it going straight away."

"Oh dear, I can't do anything right today," thought Little Owl as he went inside.

He opened the back of the clock and there was a big paper bag.

"The eggs! I've found the eggs!" he shouted and rushed out to his friends, who were very pleased to see them at last.

Everyone decided there had been enough hunting for one day, so they just shared the eggs out there and then.

When Mrs Owl found out what had happened she smiled at Little Owl and said, "It's a good thing you didn't put them inside the grandfather clock. That only needs winding once a year!"

Little Owl's Garden

Little Owl had always wanted a garden of his own where he could grow some flowers, but Mr Owl was much more keen on growing vegetables. Whenever Little Owl planted a few flowers they seemed to get covered up by cabbages or squashed by marrows.

He had more or less given up growing things until one spring when there was a very windy spell in Hollyholt.

"It sounds terrible out there tonight," said Mrs Owl, one evening. "I'm worried about that wobbly chimney pot. I knew we should have done something about it."

"I expect it will be all right," said Mr Owl. "I'll fly up and check in the morning."

But by the morning it was too late. There was a big crash in the night and Mrs Owl knew that the chimney pot had come down.

Next morning Little Owl went out to look. There was the chimney pot—it had landed right in the middle of Mr Owl's vegetables and, by some magic, it hadn't so much as squashed a Brussels sprout.

"That was lucky," said Mr Owl. "I don't think we'll put that old

pot back up there. I'll go and buy a new one today."

While Mr Owl was out Little Owl had an idea. He thought he would ask Mrs Owl about it.

"Don't you think the chimney pot would look rather good left where it is and filled with flowers?" he asked her.

"I think that's a splendid idea!" said Mrs Owl. "A few flowers would brighten up that green vegetable patch beautifully."

So Little Owl filled the chimney pot with earth and planted some bright pansies in the top of it. From then on he didn't have to worry about his flowers getting covered up or squashed because they were always way above the vegetables, safe in their tall chimney-pot garden!

The Parcel Mix-up

"My oh my, I don't know what to do next!" said Mrs Badger in a bit of a fluster. "I'm so busy today."

"Can I do anything to help?" asked Ricky Fox, who had popped in to buy his comic.

"That would be kind," said Mrs Badger. "I do have some parcels that need delivering."

Mrs Badger gave him two parcels, one for Mr Toad which he put under his left arm, and one for Mrs Duck which he put under his right arm and off he went, skipping happily until suddenly he tripped over a big stone and both his parcels went flying.

He moved the stone so no one else would trip over it and then picked up the parcels again.

When he had delivered them both, he went back to Mrs Badger's to see if there was anything else he could do to help.

"Help?" said Mrs Badger crossly. "I've just had Mrs Duck on the phone complaining that I sent her paintbrushes instead of the lace frills that she asked for. No doubt Mr Toad will phone up any moment."

"I'm sorry, I must have mixed them up," said Ricky. "I'll go and change them over right away!"

He hurried to Mr Toad's house to collect Mrs Duck's lace.

"Come in, come in," said Mr Toad. "Let me show you what I've done with that lovely lace you brought me."

Mr Toad had put Mrs Duck's lace frills across the top of all his windows.

"Don't they look pretty?" he asked Ricky. "But I still need my paintbrushes, you know. I've got to get on with the decorating."

Ricky hurried on to Mrs Duck's house to collect the paintbrushes.

"Have you brought my lace?" she asked. "Never mind, come in and see what I'm doing. Those paintbrushes gave me a good idea."

Mrs Duck had started decorating her bedroom.

"But I still need some lace to finish the dress I was making," she told Ricky.

So poor Ricky had to go back to Mrs Badger's again to collect two more parcels.

"Don't mix them up this time," said Mrs Badger with a laugh. And this time he didn't.

Fathers' Day

"You know it's Fathers' Day tomorrow, don't you?" Mrs Owl asked Little Owl. "Have you got a present ready?"

"I'm going to *make* a present," said Little Owl and he took out Mrs Owl's recipe book. He turned to chestnut chip cookies, Mr Owl's favourite, and then began to look for all the things he needed. "200 grams of flour," read Little Owl. "I don't suppose it needs to be exactly right," and he tipped half the bag of flour into a bowl. "Two eggs." He threw them straight in, shells and all, and then added a handful of chestnuts, too. He poured in some milk to mix it all together.

"It looks a bit lumpy," he thought. "And there's a lot of it. Never mind!"

Little Owl put big dollops of the mixture onto a baking tray and then called his mummy to put it in the oven.

A few minutes later Little Owl smelt a nice cooking smell in the kitchen.

"Do you think they're ready?" he asked his mummy.

"Let's go and have a look," she said and they went back to the kitchen. "Oh no!" she cried as she walked through the door.

There was a sticky brown mixture oozing out of the oven.

"I *thought* I'd made too much," said Little Owl.

22

Mrs Owl carefully opened the oven. Little Owl's cookies didn't look like cookies at all. There was just a bubbling, oozing, brown, sticky mess!

"What am I going to do?" cried Little Owl. "There's no time to make any more before Daddy gets home."

"Have you any money in your money box?" asked Mrs Owl. "If you hurry you've just got time to get to Hollyholt Stores before it closes."

The next day Mr Owl was very pleased with his present.

"Mmmm," he said, as he crunched a cookie. "These chestnut chip cookies are good. Thank you, Little Owl. Did you make them yourself?"

"Well . . . almost," said Little Owl, looking at his mummy. Then they both burst out laughing as they told Mr Owl the whole story.

Little Owl's Guitar

"Do stop making that horrible noise," moaned Tootie Owl, standing at Little Owl's bedroom door.

"I've got to practise my guitar for the school concert," said Little Owl, and he carried on playing.

"I'm fed up with hearing that thing," complained Mr Owl to Mrs Owl at dinnertime. "I wish he'd find somewhere else to play it."

Poor Little Owl! Nobody liked listening to his guitar.

One afternoon Mrs Owl told him that he couldn't play because Mrs Bunny was leaving baby Bunnikins with them and the baby wouldn't sleep with all that noise.

"All right, Mummy. I'll take it outside," he said and off he went.

Mrs Bunny arrived and left Bunnikins with Mrs Owl. She tucked her up in Tootie's old cradle and left her to sleep, but almost at once the baby started to cry.

Mrs Owl tried rocking her in her wings, Tootie bounced her on

her knee and they both sang songs, but nothing would stop the baby from crying.

Just then Little Owl appeared. "It's raining outside. Is it all right if I play my guitar in here?" he asked.

"Well there's so much noise already, a bit more can't matter," said Mrs Owl.

When Little Owl started to play, Bunnikins stopped crying for a moment and looked round to see where the music was coming from. She watched Little Owl with her bright eyes and started to gurgle a babyish sort of laugh.

"She likes it!" said Tootie. "She's laughing!"

When Mrs Bunny came to collect Bunnikins, she found her bouncing up and down in time to Little Owl's music.

"At last we've found someone who likes listening to Little Owl's guitar," said Tootie, laughing.

Bunnikins gave a happy-sounding gurgle and Little Owl beamed.

The Big Catch

"It's too hot to do anything!" moaned Nippy Shrew one morning.

"Why don't we go fishing?" suggested Little Bunny. "It will be cooler by the stream."

"Good idea!" said Nippy and he ran home to fetch his rod.

They were soon sitting under the shady willow trees beside the stream. All around them fish were jumping out of the water, but

not one came anywhere near the fishing lines.

"Fishing's boring," said Little Bunny, who was tired of waiting for something to happen. "Why don't we . . ."

Just then he felt a tug on his line and he almost went head-over-heels into the water.

"Quick, Nippy!" he shouted. "Give me a hand!" They both pulled as hard as they could.

"It must be a big one!" said Little Bunny excitedly. "One more pull." They pulled again and suddenly they toppled backwards. Nippy squeaked as Little Bunny landed on top of him.

When they sat up they couldn't believe what they saw. There on the end of Little Bunny's line was a battered old kettle, full of holes.

"All that pulling for nothing!" moaned Little Bunny.

"It's great!" said Nippy. "Just what I need."

"Don't be silly! Whatever can you do with an old kettle?"

"Come round to my house this afternoon and you'll find out," answered Nippy, with a grin. "And bring your swimming trunks."

That afternoon as Little Bunny walked up to Nippy's house he could hear a lot of splashing. There was Nippy in his swimming trunks with a lovely shower of water falling all over him.

"Do you like my shower?" he asked. Nippy had hung the old kettle from a tree and pushed the garden hose into the spout. Water poured from all the holes in the kettle.

"Great!" said Little Bunny. "This is the best way to spend a hot afternoon."

New Wellingtons

It had been raining hard and the garden was full of puddles. Little Owl thought it would be fun to splash about a bit so he hunted through the jumbled pile of boots and shoes in the cupboard until he found his wellingtons. He had quite a struggle to pull them on and when he stood up they pinched his toes.

"I've grown out of them," he said. "Bother! I can't go splashing in puddles until I get some new ones."

Mrs Owl had some shopping to do in Hollyholt so she took Little Owl with her to buy some new boots. The first pair he tried was too big. The next pair was too small. Another pair was too narrow and some others were too wide.

By the time Little Owl had found a comfortable pair the shop floor was covered with boots.

"It'll take some time to sort them out into the right pairs," said

Mrs Owl, as they left the shop. "Still, if you're happy . . ."

She suddenly realized that Little Owl was no longer walking beside her. She turned round and there he was, flat on the ground in the middle of a puddle!

"Do look where you're going," said Mrs Owl, helping him up and trying to wipe off some of the mud. "You'd better hold on to me so you don't fall over again."

They went a bit further and Little Owl suddenly fell forwards, almost pulling Mrs Owl with him.

"What *is* the matter with you?" she asked.

"I keep treading on my toes," said Little Owl. "I don't seem to be able to walk properly."

"It must be those boots," said Mrs Owl. "Though I'd have thought that after trying so many on you should have found a pair that fitted you."

They went straight back to the shop. They found the assistant sitting in the middle of the floor surrounded by all the boots that Little Owl had tried.

"I'm trying to sort them into pairs," she told them. "But no matter how I do it, I always end up with one pair that has two right feet."

"There's something wrong with *my* boots, too," said Little Owl.

They all looked carefully at his boots. Suddenly Mrs Owl understood. "You've been wearing two left boots," she said, laughing. "No wonder you kept falling over!"

Skippy's Kite

Little Bunny's cousin Skippy had come to stay at the Bunnies' house, all by herself. She was rather shy, and Benny and Little Bunny didn't think she would be much fun to play with.

They sat outside on the step, wondering what they could do.

"I wish we had some roller skates," said Benny, "or a bike."

"We could fly my kite," suggested Skippy.

"A kite! Great!" shouted Benny and Little Bunny together.

When they saw the kite, though, they went quiet. It was a home-made, paper one.

"I made it myself," explained Skippy.

"I thought it would be a big one with a long tail, like Little Owl's," said Little Bunny.

Benny frowned at him. "I'm sure it flies just as well. Come on."

Soon they were on top of the hill. Little Owl was there too, with his smart new kite. He laughed when he saw Skippy's.

"You won't get anywhere with that," he cried. "You need a real kite, like mine."

Little Owl let out the string and threw his kite into the sky. It soared nicely, floating high above the hill.

After a few minutes, Skippy and the Bunnies got their kite going too. Up it went, alongside Little Owl's. The two flew side by side until, all of a sudden, the wind dropped. Instead of the lovely gusts, there was just a tiny, gentle breeze.

It wasn't enough to keep Little Owl's kite in the air, and it fell like a stone, crashing on the grass. The Bunnies' kite was still flying high and Little Owl looked sad. Skippy went over to him.

"Would you like me to show you how to make a paper kite?" she asked. "They are much better on days like this when there isn't much wind. Your kite is really for very windy days when paper ones get torn to shreds."

"All right, then, thanks," said Little Owl, beginning to cheer up. "Why don't you all come round to my house and we'll make one now?"

So that is what they did. Soon there were two home-made kites flying high above the hill. And the next time it was very windy, they all went out with Little Owl to take turns with *his* kite.

A Spot of Trouble For Little Owl

"Tomorrow," said Mr Mole, "we shall have a counting test."

"Oh no!" thought Little Owl. "I'm no good at counting." He flew home feeling miserable.

"Cheer up," said Tootie Owl. "I'll help you learn your numbers."

"No," said Little Owl. "There's too many. I'll just have to stay at home."

Next morning Little Owl didn't appear at breakfast.

"Whatever's the matter with him?" asked Mrs Owl and she went to find out. Little Owl was covered in red spots.

"Gracious!" she exclaimed. "Look at those spots! I'll call the doctor at once!"

Dr Hare soon arrived. He examined Little Owl and smiled.

"What are you missing at school today?" he asked.

"Counting test," said Little Owl, in his weakest voice.

"Ha! I thought so," said the Doctor, winking at Mrs Owl. "Give him two teaspoons of this medicine every hour," he instructed, handing over a bottle of black syrup. "It's extract of bladderwrack. I think you'll find the spots disappear very quickly." He chuckled as he left.

Mrs Owl gave Little Owl his first dose. It tasted horrible. As soon as she left the room he grabbed his hanky and scrubbed at his painted spots. But they wouldn't come off!

So Little Owl had to take his horrible medicine every hour until it was bath time and the spots washed away.

The next time there was a counting test Little Owl made sure he knew *all* his numbers!

The School Fête

Grandma Squirrel was carefully dusting the windowsill when, suddenly, a pot fell off and landed with a crack on the floor. It was one of Grandpa Squirrel's plant pots with a bright red geranium in it.

"It's no good," Grandma told Grandpa. "There are just too many plants in this house. I can't even do the dusting without knocking one off. Some of them will have to go."

This was very hard for Grandpa Squirrel, who was very fond of his plants and was always growing new ones. He could quite understand that there were too many in the house and he didn't

mind getting rid of some, but he didn't want to throw them away. He couldn't put any more in the greenhouse, because that was already full. He was still worrying about it when Little Squirrel arrived for tea.

"It's the school fête next week," she told them. "There will be stalls selling cakes, stalls with games, and some races too. Little Mouse and I want to have a stall but we can't think of anything that we could sell. Have you got any ideas?"

Grandpa smiled broadly. "Yes, I have," he said. "You can sell geraniums. I've been growing far too many and I don't know what to do with them all."

"Thanks, Grandpa, that *is* a good idea," said Little Squirrel.

On the day of the school fête Grandpa and Little Squirrel

walked down into Hollyholt with Grandpa's wheelbarrow piled high with plants. The stall was such a success that Grandpa had to go back for some more in the afternoon.

On Monday morning Mr Mole walked into the classroom looking very happy.

"You will be pleased to hear that we raised a lot of money at the school fête," he told them. "In fact, we raised enough to be able to buy all the new books we want for the school library, and some plants for the school garden as well. We can get sunflowers, roses —and some nice red geraniums."

When she heard that, Little Squirrel couldn't help chuckling.

35

The Fire Engine

Mr and Mrs Owl had been to town to do some shopping. They arrived home looking very pleased with themselves.

"Just look at this shiny wheelbarrow!" said Mr Owl. "It'll be a lot better than the old, rusty one with the wobbly wheel."

"And what about this alarm clock?" said Mrs Owl. "Now we'll be able to get up on time. The old one was always slow."

"Can I have all the old things?" asked Little Owl.

"What *are* you going to do with an old wheelbarrow and an alarm clock?" asked Mr Owl. "Of course you can have them!"

Little Owl rushed up to the bedroom to fetch the old alarm clock, then he found some string and his paints and went down to the garden shed, where the wheelbarrow was kept.

Tootie could hardly wait to see what Little Owl was making. At last he opened the shed door.

"There," he said. "What do you think of my fire engine?"

He had painted the sides of the wheelbarrow red and tied the alarm clock to the handle. Tootie climbed in and Little Owl wound up the alarm so that it rang as they went round the garden.

"This is fun!" said Tootie. "I wish we had a fire to put out."

Mr Owl came to see what all the noise was about.

"You can pretend the daisies are on fire," he told Tootie, handing her the watering can. "And you can put them out! That will save me from watering the garden today."

So Mr Owl pottered about in his shed while Tootie and Little Owl took turns in the fire engine until they had watered all the flowers.

Little Owl's Hiccups

"Hic!" went Little Owl at breakfast one morning.

"Oh dear," said Mrs Owl. "You've got hiccups. Drink a glass of water."

Little Owl tried that but he still kept hiccuping between mouthfuls of toast.

"Try drinking from the wrong side of the glass," said Mr Owl.

Little Owl tried that and spilt water all over himself, so he had to go and change. Mrs Owl got cross with Mr Owl for suggesting something so silly.

"At least it worked," said Mr Owl, but just then Little Owl came back into the kitchen and went 'hic!' once again.

"What you have to do," said Tootie, "is hold your nose while you drink a glass of water."

"If I drink much more water I'll burst," said Little Owl, but he tried it anyway. It didn't work.

"I can't go to school with hiccups," he said.

"Well you can't stay at home for something like that," said Mrs Owl. "You'll just have to get rid of them on the way there."

Little Owl set off for school and asked everyone he met if they knew a cure for hiccups. They *all* did!

"Stand on your head," said Little Bunny.

"Hold your breath and count to thirty," said Little Squirrel.

"Put an acorn down your back," said Percy Woodpecker.

Little Owl tried them all, but none of them worked.

"Mr Mole will be cross if I hiccup all day," thought Little Owl miserably, as he went into the classroom.

"Good morning, everyone," said Mr Mole. "Now, you all wrote a story last night for homework. Today I'd like you to read your stories to the rest of the class. Stand up, Little Owl, and you can begin."

What a shock for Little Owl! He had forgotten all about his homework and so he had nothing to read. Of course, Mr Mole wasn't very pleased and he said Little Owl had to stay in at playtime to write his story.

"Cheer up, Little Owl," whispered Tootie kindly. "At least your hiccups have gone—everyone knows the best cure is a big shock!"

The Last Swallow

Mrs Bunny was woken early by a lot of noise outside the bedroom window. She jumped out of bed and opened the curtains.

There was a small swallow hopping about and chirping loudly. He looked rather lost so Mrs Bunny put on her dressing gown and slippers and went outside.

"I've lost my mummy and daddy," wailed the swallow. "And my brothers and sisters too. They all flew from the nest, but when I tried to follow I just landed on the ground. I can't fly." And he started to sob.

"Don't worry," said Mrs Bunny. "I can't fly, but I manage very nicely. You can come and stay with us."

Little Bunny and Benny were delighted to have a new friend and Swoop, the swallow, fitted in very well, once he'd got used to eating carrot crunchies for breakfast. After a few days Mrs Bunny thought it would be a good idea for Swoop to go to school with the others, so off he went.

Mr Mole was surprised to see him. "You shouldn't be here," he said. "All the swallows have gone."

"Gone where?" asked Swoop.

"Every year at this time swallows travel south to a hot country far away where they spend the winter. Our winters are too cold for swallows."

"But I don't want to go," said Swoop. "I'm happy living with the Bunnies—and besides, I can't fly."

But Mr Mole was very firm. "You'll have to learn," he said. "Little Owl will help."

So Little Owl spent the morning teaching Swoop to fly. At first he couldn't even get off the ground (swallows always find that hard), but gradually he got better and he surprised Mrs Bunny when he flew right into the house that afternoon.

"I'm going to find my friends," he explained. "Thank you for letting me stay."

Mrs Bunny smiled and waved as he flew off. "Come and see us again next summer," she called.

Nutting

It was autumn. The leaves were falling fast and chestnuts were starting to fall too.

"Let's go nutting at the weekend," suggested Little Squirrel one playtime. "We'll see who can find the biggest chestnut."

So on Saturday Little Squirrel, Little Mouse, Timmy and Tom Prickles set off with baskets on their arms.

"Let's start here," said Little Mouse, pointing to a big, old tree.

They collected lots of chestnuts from under it and then they wandered off a little way to find some more. They hunted about in the crinkly, brown leaves, all hoping to find the biggest nut. When their baskets were full they met under the big tree.

"Shall we see who's got the biggest?" said Little Squirrel.

"We're not all here yet," said Little Mouse. "Where's Tom Prickles?"

They all called, "Tom" at the tops of their voices, but there was no reply.

"We'd better go and look for him," said Little Squirrel. They set off in different directions, calling his name as they went. Tom was nowhere to be found.

Suddenly, Timmy shouted, "Look, everyone!"

"Have you found Tom?" asked the others, running up to him.

"No," said Timmy. "But I have found the biggest chestnut. It's huge!"

They all went to look. There it was, sticking out from under a pile of leaves, a big, prickly, brown chestnut.

"I wonder how many there are inside?" said Timmy, reaching out to pick it up.

Just then it moved and Timmy screamed, "It's alive!"

The chestnut slowly stood up, shaking off some of the fallen leaves, and Little Squirrel started to laugh. "No wonder your chestnut was so big, Timmy. It wasn't a chestnut at all, it was Tom Prickles—having a snooze!"

The Amazing Talking Snowman

One morning Little Mouse woke up and looked out of her window to find that it had been snowing all night.

"Timmy, it's snowing! It's snowing!" she cried, running into his room and waking him up. "Let's make a snowman!"

They dressed quickly and were soon busily scooping snow into a big pile. They had just about finished making the body when Timmy had an idea.

"Let's make it a really special snowman," he said. "We'll make it talk!"

Little Mouse didn't see how you could make a snowman talk, but Timmy was sure he could and he had soon set up his trick.

"It will surprise all our friends," he laughed, as they gave the snowman a hat, a carrot nose and two chestnuts for eyes.

Just then Little Owl walked past and Timmy decided to try out the snowman.

"You call him into the garden. I'll make the snowman talk," he whispered to Little Mouse.

Little Owl laughed when Little Mouse explained about the talking snowman, but he said he'd have a look. As he walked up to it, the snowman suddenly spoke in a deep, hollow voice.

"Hello, Little Owl."

Little Owl nearly jumped out of his feathers. "It really does talk!" he cried, and he began to ask it questions until it was time to go to school.

In the classroom, Little Owl told everyone about the amazing snowman. They all asked Little Mouse if they could come and see

it and she told them to come straight after school.

It was a lovely sunny day as they tramped back to Little Mouse's house. Timmy ran on ahead to get ready to play his trick again and he felt quite hot by the time he reached home. He dashed into the garden shed to wait for the others.

Soon everyone was gathered round the snowman, whispering and giggling with excitement.

"Hello, hello, hello," said the snowman, slowly. Just then, Benny Bunny pointed to the snowman's carrot nose which was sliding down its face. "The snowman's melting!" he cried.

The snowman *was* melting, very quickly—and so was the snow on the ground. And, as it did so, the schoolfriends noticed Mr Mouse's green garden hose, leading from the snowman's mouth all the way to the shed.

They followed the hose into the shed, where they saw Timmy Mouse talking down it, pretending to be the snowman. Poor Timmy! He'd been found out, and everyone teased him for a long time afterwards about the amazing, *melting* snowman.